MUSINGS OF THE GIRL NEXT DOOR

A Collection of Poerty and Insight

Melissa Parker

Kindle Direct Publishing

ISBN: 9798746631862

Cover design by: Kindle Creator
Library of Congress Control Number: 2021909052
Printed in the United States of America

*This book is dedicated to all my loved ones, both living and deceased.
Without you, I would not be the woman I am today.*

CONTENTS

INTRODUCTION

The poems in this book are arranged alphabetically and were written over a span of 25 years. Over the years, I have been inspired by beautiful scenery, dreams, nightmares, heartache, loss, love, faith, hope, etc. This is not the book I imagined it would be when I started so many years ago. Though I hope it is better as it shares a bit of my soul with the world.

Aged By Time

Be still my heart
I have found lost love,

It blossoms within
Though aged by time,

One wicked smile
Was all it took,

"I love thee" and
"I love thou,"

These are just spoken words
But does love truly endure?

My heart cries out
But no one is there,

You said goodbye
But life is not fair,

As the years go on
My love holds fast,

The hands of time
Go round and round,

My love is thine
From sky to ground.

Along The Way

A rose is a rose
A thorn is a thorn,

Please mend my heart
Where it has torn,

Day to day I find my way
Love is not here to stay,

As years go by
Life passes me by,

I've found some happiness along the path
I long to share with the boy from my past,

We talked and laughed
We kissed and laughed,

Made plans for the future
But 'twas not meant to be,

You now have what you wanted
A wife
A child
But who asked what I wanted?

My dreams are simple and true
But they can no longer include you.

At The Crossroads

Here at the crossroads
Many roads converge
Which way do I turn?
I feel I'm on the verge

Behind me lay piles of rubble
Blocking the once tread path
Remembering all of the trouble
Determined to keep it in the past

Looking ahead with anticipation
Life as I know it is ending
The Lord issued me an invitation
Today marks a new beginning

Looking ahead toward unfamiliar road
I quiver in my new running shoes
When I can't go on, He'll carry my load
Forging ahead with so much to lose

I bow to You Lord with all that I am
Please Lord show me the way
I continue on, doing the best I can
Loving You more every day.

Beauty

The sky shades blue
The air grows crisp,

What beauty here
Did I almost miss?

Thin wispy clouds sail majestically by
As kids fly kites to soaring heights,

Waves rush in like a lion's roar
As seagulls fly to a boat's moor,

The sun sets in the western sky
Rays of light dance brilliantly in the sky,

Colors such as I have never seen
Paint God's canvas blue and green,

With red and yellow grow seas of fire
Blue and purple streak higher and higher,

And then the stars of heavenly night
Speckle the sky with their bright light,

What beauty here did God's hand make?
For all to love and not forsake!

Faith

What is Faith?

Faith is the hope that guides you
Through this hell called Life,

Faith is love for the unseen
Angels are all around us,

Faith is what makes us whole
God's true gift of Love,

Faith is what we all possess
Though many do deny it,

Faith may come in many forms
A child's Faith pure and true,

Faith will never fail God's children
Through God your Faith will save you.

Forever

The day grows dim
My heart grows heavy,

I think of him
I'm not too steady,

The little boy that once ran free
Never once came back to me,

I hold on to what he left behind
Truth is there's not much left to find,

Life goes on as they say
My heart grows colder day by day,

The loneliness overwhelms me
I question if he ever loved me,

My heart betrays me ever still
I think I'll love him until the End,

Forever seems so long and grim
Will I ever belong to him?

No.

Hope Remains

Hope remains in the dead of night
When all is dark and silent
Life lays still and dormant
A flower not yet in bloom

Darkness creeps across the land
Slithering in all directions
Smothering all living things
Possessing all in its path

The air thickens and shimmers
As dark gives way to light
Radiating through the darkness
Bursting from the depths of night

Moments pass as night becomes day
Darkness temporarily defeated
Basking in God's great glory
Welcoming the dawn of a new day

How Long Will Love Survive?

She appears in a veil of shimmering light
One solitary tear running down her silky cheek,

She talks of passion and love that smolders and burns
When true love takes its grip on unsuspecting souls,

She once had love within her grasp
But fear of love's intensity turned her away,

The man who loved her above all else
Cursed her with longing and loneliness for centuries,

Only true love could break this morbid curse
The love of three couples was the only way,

Fate took its course with the help of two lost souls
They worked their magic through lofty dreams,

And one by one lost souls began to love
But the job was not fully completed,

For two headstrong and stubborn souls refused the lure
As the ancient tortured souls helplessly looked on,

And then love attacked with unwavering accuracy
The curse was broken,

She dried her tears and opened her heart
To the fire and passion she should never have feared.

Inconceivable

An inconceivable threat ravages us today. The world today is not the same world that existed yesterday. People are sick and dying. Loved ones gone in the blink of an eye with no end in sight. This plague does not discriminate against age, race, weight, gender, religion, sexuality, or any other category that could be named. No one knows who it will be next and why kills some but not others. Logic and reasoning do not apply. The road ahead will not be easy. Rebuilding is only possible if we work together. Those who can help have a responsibility to do so. No matter your beliefs, we all must come together and help in any way we can... money, services, support, prayer, volunteering, etc. No contribution is too small as it is the intent and effort behind it that counts. Can we put our differences aside and work together to make the world a safer and better place? We will make it through these trying times but what will the world look like when all is said and done? United we will stand against the monsters that plague us. For we are more than our loss, our pain, our uncertainty, our fear, and our fragile humanity. Our strength and resilience make us a worthy foe. Take heart and know you are one among many who will win this battle. You are not alone.

Independence Day

Independence Day is more than a day in history. It is a day when we choose which side we are on...right or wrong...good or evil. It is our choices that make us who we are. Do we turn to Him and his infinite wisdom or do we turn away, struggling in the midst of barely contained chaos, alone? Our choices affect the outcome. We choose the easy or rocky road. Sometimes the easy path is the hardest path, though it may be smooth for a time, the lesson impacts with jarring force. For to learn and progress, we must go through these trials. The key is our freedom to choose. Freedom to pray and worship. Freedom to rejoice in His love and freedom to walk away. Freedom to enjoy life and freedom to suffer. Suffering is not His choice, but our choice to punish ourselves. Suffering beyond our control is used as a life lesson. It is our choice to prolong it or surrender ourselves to Him. He will carry our burdens when we cannot bear them; and carry us when cannot go on. For each new day is our Independence Day. We declare our freedom in the choices we make. Independent does not mean alone. Independence with God is the ultimate freedom.

Life Is Nothing Without Love

Life is precious and fragile
Seductive in its joys
Bewitching despite its flaws
Treacherous in its innocence
Manipulative yet beguiling
Agonizing in its intensity
Devastating in its complexity
Yet fleeting and fickle
Life is nothing without Love
Love is debilitating in its purity
Restorative to the soul
Treacherous in its blindness
Yet love gives purpose, meaning, and joy
Renewing the hopeless
Breathing life into the dead
Without love, I have nothing

Life

I drift along the path of life
Winding my way through twists and turns,

The warmth of the sun surrounding me
I must be careful as not to burn,

I bask in the sun's great glory
And then the ride begins again,

Going faster and faster
But there is no end,

And then the warmth turns to bitter cold
As death once again shows its ugly face,

I continue forward though I cannot go on
My heart breaking with each new day,

And then the sun comes again to play
I long to bloom in its glorious rays,

Life seems too good to take for granted
I count my blessings night and day,

The journey through life is long and treacherous
But only a few learn the lessons that surround us,

Will this wonderful warmth last very long?
We know not what we have until it is gone!

Longing

I look across the rolling hills
And all I feel is fire,

I see his face in my dreams
The object of my desire,

I long to feel his sweet embrace
To feel the warmth of his love,

I long to be in his bright future
I long to provide his children,

I long to be his devoted wife
And love him until the end,

I long to hold him in my arms
And nuzzle him there forever,

I long to laugh and share his life
And love him forever as his wife,

I long to grow old with him day after day
I long to die together,

I long to be content with today
We'll be together forever someday.

Love Flows Abundantly

Today I saw a friend at Target
She startled me in her exuberance,
Surprising me with a great big hug
Today I feel Loved.

Today I saw a friend at Wal-Mart
He was too far to greet safely,
So I watched from afar with fondness
Today I feel Loved.

Today I researched science project ideas
Choosing several then narrowing down to one,
Tornados are my daughter's interest
Today I feel Loved.

Today I attended Saturday night service
Letting the music wash over me,
Hearing the words resonate in my heart
Today I feel Loved.

Today I said, "Thank You, Lord"
Feeling peace flow throughout me,
Knowing He will provide all my needs
His love flows abundantly.

Mary

To my daughter Mary, we will be together again someday.

I hold you dear
Inside my heart,

So sweet and small
And bold at heart,

You taught me love
You showed me pain,

I think of you
You left too soon,

I love you now for eternity
I pray one day you'll come back for me,

Once life seemed so dull and grim
I'm grateful for the short time we had,

I now know love and life
I promise to live a happy life,

I owe this all to you
Mary, my sweet angel.

May God Bless You

Love
Like a rose in bloom unfolding its petals,

Beauty
A sterling rose so flawless to the eye,

Joy
It grows and grows creating a glow within,

Peace
It warms and flows like a calm ocean breeze,

Sadness
A cold chill that creeps upon you,

Loneliness
A dark cold room with no way to escape,

Faith
The knowledge you're never truly alone,

Blessed
A heavenly state only bestowed by God.

You are a blessed child of God.

Morning Glory

I open my eyes every morning
My thoughts plan the day

I see the sun's bright glory
But there are no words to say

I stand and stretch, touch the sky
And bend down low, touch my toes

I stand in the shower, steam rising up
Water runs down cleansing my soul

I think of him every morning
And dream of him every night

I see him in my thoughts and dreams
And wish for my own shining knight

My Precious Child

My precious child
So small and young,
Why do you hide?
Not accepting My Love

My precious child
So lost and scared,
Why do you run?
When your soul is bared?

My precious child
So full of promise,
Where is your faith in Me?
Never feeling My kiss?

My precious child
So full of hope,
When will you hear Me?
Near the end of your rope?

My precious child
I await you in Heaven,
The joy of My heart
The gifts I have given.

My precious child
Know I love you dearly,
With bated breath
When you see Me clearly.

My precious child
So full of love,
Are you calling for Me?
I will wait for you there.

In the quiet morning hours
Any day of the week,
Simply call out to Me

My precious child.

My Uncle Jay

A gentle man so strong and sure
Loved by all who knew him
Left the world with silent grace
A heart of gold, so pure

Though he's gone forevermore
His presence lingers still
In the hearts of those he loved
Wandering through the hills

And in the quiet early morn
He stands beside the crick
Listening so intently
To the water and its secrets

Though all we have are memories
Your love remains, my friend
You will never be forgotten
I love you and this is not the end.

This poem is dedicated to my giant teddy bear. I am sorry I could not say goodbye but I will see you again someday. Go with my love and know that you will be missed.

Peace

I stand alone on the seashore
Wondering what I could do more,

Waves rush in as birds take flight
My heart soars free on this bright night,

Light dances from wave to wave
Playing a silent symphony,

My hair stirs in the gentle breeze
How long will I feel at peace?

I feel the tranquility of this night
Peace flows through me on this very night,

My heart grows softer day to day
My soul fears not the end of the day,

If only peace would live forever
The world could love and come together.

Prayer, Faith, Hope & Love

I pray for those who are lost
I pray for those in pain,

I pray for God to heal my broken family
I pray for God to heal my broken heart,

Faith is all I have in this world
Faith that my Father will take care of me,

Faith that what doesn't kill me will make me stronger
Faith that my Father will bring me home someday,

Hope that I will live a happy and full life
Hope that I do not fail my Father,

Love all things without prejudice or hatred
Love those who make love seem impossible,

You must love yourself before you can truly love others
And above all, love thy Father for He will provide for all your needs.

Silence

The hour is late, I am alone again
Darkness deepens, my heart grows heavy

I see you in my thoughts and dreams
Happy yet fragmented pieces

My heart beats in ardent discord
Squeezed by an invisible force

I call out your name, but no one is there
Silence answers with deafening force

Memories haunt me like old lost friends
Blackness surrounds me, I see what was

Ghosts from my past whirling endlessly
My heart seizes, seeing you there

Falling to my knees, crying out your name
Weeping my soul into oblivion

Shattered pieces of all I have been
Frozen in unyielding silence

Song From Within

I hear that familiar melody
The song that seems to emanate from within,

It seems so familiar yet so strange
Does my heart really sing that tune?

It calls to me like an old lost friend
And folds me in its overwhelming warmth,

I hear the chords in my thoughts and dreams
It touches the very center of my soul,

I long to dance and play and love
It sets me free from even the deepest sorrow,

It calls to me with its ever-changing chords
With highs and lows and a sound that's unreal,

Could something so beautiful really come from me?
Deep feelings rising and falling with each beautiful note,

Words cannot express what my song sings
Beauty, love, joy, sadness. . .Just aren't enough!

I dream of finding a song that echoes mine
Would I dream that it were possible,

Everyone sings his or her own unique song
In hopes of finding that one special echo.

Space

The sun sets in the western sky
Signaling the end of the day,

The moon comes out in its white glory
Willing the stars to play,

I look beyond the earth's thin shield
And into the depths of space,

Passing clouds of dust and gas
And balls of fire finding their place,

Stars like none I've ever seen
Burn and age with time,

Stars that come in pairs of two
And stars as black as night,

But is there really life out there
In the void called space?

Man feels very lonely
Thinking there's no one else,

Man is very arrogant
Thinking he's alone,

For if Earth holds the only life
It's an awful waste of space.

Surrender

Here I am again Lord,
Humble before you now,

Laying my heart at your feet.
To my knees I fall,

Throwing my burdens down,
Seeing them turn to dust.

Surrendering all I am,
Entrusting my life to You,

I'm Yours to command Lord
Take all of me and make it Yours,

Use me for Your will alone,
Living for You is the only way.

All I have, all I am, and all I will become is yours now and forever.

The Ancient Song

Emerald green hills roll on and on
As far as the eye can see,

I feel the magic in the cool crisp air
And smell the salt of the sea,

I hear the land as it sings to me
The ancient old song of love and loss,

I feel the old song within my heart
As I run my hand on the damp green moss,

I travel back to the time of old
When knights still wore shining armor,

I feel strange and fuzzy inside
Knowing something will happen once more,

And then I see his smiling face
The man of my dreams where love lives forever,

I long to feel his sweet embrace
But he disappears and vanishes forever,

The fog rolls in and the green hills turn to gray
As the day comes to an end and the sky turns to black,

Was he really a dream of my present day longing?
Or will the magic of the land bring him right back?

The Blackness

The blackness surrounds me in suffocating strength
Panic rises from the core of my being

I cannot draw air deep into my lungs
Will this be the end of me?

Pain engulfs me as my heart is mangled
I feel so alone in this overwhelming blackness

Wait, is that a sliver of light I see?
Hope blooms anew from deep within

And then I see him, holding his hand out to me
I reach towards the light and the love he brings

His smile fades as we drift farther apart
I run towards him but not able to reach him

I feel the cold sadness seeping inside me again
Running faster and faster to no avail

I call out to him with all my being
Seeing tears sliding down his cheeks

I sink deeper and deeper into the black abyss
Oh why can't I reach him?

Will I ever see his smiling face again?
Or will the blackness claim yet another soul?

The Dance

Standing proud I begin my dance
Swaying gently in the breeze,

I stretch my arms far and wide
Waving them towards the sea,

I bend and stretch with all my glory
Performing so gracefully,

The wind calls to me with furious force
Making my movements faster,

I bend and wave at a frantic pace
And then I just dance faster,

And when the wind begins to calm
Hearing my desperate plea,

I rest again, standing tall and proud
Waiting for my next dance by the sea.

The Message

The road is long and treacherous
Lives lost everyday
Rain slicked like the river
Smooth as panes of glass
Above the posted limit
Speeders drive the track
Lights of brilliant red
Continue to light the way
Breaks screech in horror
Cars spin every which way
Landing in the ditch somewhere
Some flip up and down
Prayer cried out in desperate plea
God please do not let me die today
Out of the clouds the sun arrives
The answers clear as day
I will call you when I am ready child
Then I will come back for you.

The Road

I look down the road
I see where I've been

I look down the road
I see where I'm going

I walk straight ahead
But look back once in a while

Where does the road lead?
Is it straight and narrow?

Does it bend and curve?
I come to a crossroads

Do I go left or right?
Forward or back?

I must make a choice
I hope it is the right path.

Until We Meet Again

As humans we are fragile and often broken
But with God we are strong and whole

How many times do we let go when it's hard?
Hurt and alone...we lose hope in miracles

Forgetting the One who is always there.
On the verge of desperation

We sink further than ever before
But His love lifts us up and envelops us

Creating a cocoon of nourishment and peace
Temporary bliss but a moment in time

He works his magic inside and out
Emerging transformed but heart intact

Setting us on our path with a gentle nudge
Until next we meet once again.

White Wonder

Leaves of yellow and orange
Blanket the mountainside,

Streams of ice-cold water
Wind their way towards Earth,

Animals of the forest
Prepare for the coming snow,

The air grows colder day-by-day
Like a calm before the storm,

The winds begin to blow and swirl
As snowflakes dance and twirl,

I stand alone in this white wonder
Hoping the snow will pull me asunder,

Christmas approaches with steadfast haste
With holiday joys I will not partake,

I long to stay in this white wonder
Where love and joy are simple and true,

Holidays bring feelings of loss and heartache
Though family and friends help dull the pain,

I long to stay in this white wonder
In hope that someday my dreams will come true.

Who Am I?

Who am I?
A daughter
A woman
A mother

What am I?
A poet
A writer
A lover

Where have I been?
France
England
Scotland

Where am I going?
Alaska
Ireland
Italy

What Feel I?
Happy
Giddy
And Glee

What Dream I?
A husband
A family
Acceptance

What Need I?
Laughter
Honesty
And Love

This is who I am
.........what I am
.........where I have been

.........where I am going
.........what I feel
.........what I dream
.........and what I need.

Thought For The Day #1

Have you ever felt like you are being called to a higher purpose, but you have no idea what that purpose is? We all have different talents or gifts which God bestowed upon us to fulfill His master plan. Some of us are writers, artists, musicians, teachers, ministers, healers… the list goes on and on. How do you really know what your purpose is in life?

To answer this question, I have done a lot soul-searching, praying, and just trying to listen to God. I have always considered myself to be a good listener, but this has been my biggest challenge. I spend a lot of time in my car commuting to and from work. I crank up the music (Z88.3) and try to commune with God.

At first the silence was deafening…and disappointing. I thought that maybe God was angry with me for not coming to Him sooner, for ignoring Him, and for not trusting Him with my problems sooner. Needless to say, the silence did not last long, and I got the message loud and clear… "trust in Me for I am your God, and I will never fail
you."

I was finally able to give God all my problems, trust that He will take care of me, and I have been rewarded in return. Now it is my turn to give something of myself so that I can help others. I hope that sharing my life (the joy as well as the struggles) will help others, especially those of you who need to know that you are not alone out there.

There is so much going on around us in our daily lives that it is almost impossible to hear what God is saying. Please take a few moments every day to say, "Thank you" and to let Him know that you are listening.

So do not fear, for I am with you; do not be dismayed, for I am your God. I will strengthen you and help you; I will uphold you with my righteous right hand. Isaiah 41:10

Thought For The Day #2

Wow, you really can worship anywhere, even at home. I really did not plan to make this a time of worship but strangely I find myself doing exactly that. Just relax, open your heart, and let it happen.

Though For The Day #3

I find myself thanking God almost every day for small blessings...though I always want more (I cannot help it). I prayed that God would take away my worries. He hasn't taken them away but He still answered my prayer because, at the end of the day, I have a sense of peace despite my worry. I can come here, play some music, and be exactly where I need to be (spiritually).

Thank you, Lord, for blessing me in ways I never dared to hope for and may You bless my family and friends with the same abandon. Thank you for being the Father I never had here on Earth. I cannot imagine how I could possibly love You more.

Thought For The Day #4

God works and does everything in his own time. Be patient and know that it will be your time soon.

Thought For The Day #5

Life gets busy and sometimes we forget to talk to Him. It only takes a moment to close your eyes, take a deep breath, and thank Him for the good and the bad. Let His peace wash over you and know that even though you may have forgotten him...He did not forget you.

Thought For The Day #6

Only God knows your destiny, but it is up to you to decide how to get there. Your attitude dictates the difficulty or ease of the ride. Make it a good one and do not let the inconsequential things get you down.

Thought For The Day #7

Hard work and dedication bring peace and enlightenment. Do not be afraid to put in the effort and God will reward you greatly.

Thought For The Day #8

I glimpsed The Garden today. Through my struggle I found my way back to church, to old and new friends, and finally back home. I feel a connection I thought long lost. His love and words flowing through me like a river. Humble, I pray for His guidance with this gift He bestowed upon me. Once, I thought it a burden, but now I see it is a tool to help others. Though life goes on, He is never far when I need Him. His words, music, and peace wash over me when I need them most. Though the Garden is not a literal place, I glimpsed it in my heart… where hope, love, and peace thrive; where I can lay down my burdens and know He will meet all my needs. "I come to the garden alone…" Such beautiful music.

In the Garden - Song Lyrics
I come to the garden alone,
While the dew is still on the roses,
And the voice I hear falling on my ear
The Son of God discloses.

    Refrain:
    And He walks with me, and He talks with me,
    And He tells me I am His own;
    And the joy we share as we tarry there,
    None other has ever known.

He speaks, and the sound of His voice
Is so sweet the birds hush their singing,
And the melody that He gave to me
Within my heart is ringing.

I'd stay in the garden with Him,
Though the night around me be falling,
But He bids me go; through the voice of woe
His voice to me is calling.